Tyrone O'Saurus DREAMS

JAMES HOWE

illustrated by RANDY CECIL

CANDLEWICK PRESS

First edition 2021

Library of Congress Catalog Card Number pending
ISBN 978-1-5362-1087-3

20 21 22 23 24 25 TLF 10 9 8 7 6 5 4 3 2 1

Printed in Dongguan, Guangdong, China

This book was typeset in Wilke Bold.
The illustrations were done in oil.

Candlewick Press
99 Dover Street
Somerville, Massachusetts 02144

www.candlewick.com

For Carson and all the Saffers
JH

For Bud
RC

Tyrone O'Saurus had a dream.

It was not the dream his father had for him.

Tyrone did not want to be a dentist.

It was not the dream his mother had for him.
"You are so smart," she said. "You would be
an excellent lawyer."

Tyrone did not want to be a lawyer. His legs were too wiggly and jiggly to have to sit at a desk all day.

"You are quick on your feet," his brother, Johnny, said. "You should go out for football. You could be team captain. Like me. Win lots of trophies. Like me. Play in the DFL someday. Like me."

Tyrone did not want to play in the Dinosaur Football League someday. That was not his dream.

"My arms are too short to throw," he said.

"That hasn't stopped me," his brother replied. "You have to dream big and work to make your dream come true. Like—"

"You," Tyrone said. *Maybe*, he thought, *I should give up my dream and be a football star instead. Like Johnny.*

"I'll try," said Tyrone.

"Go for it!" Johnny said.

Tyrone got stronger.

But he didn't get better.

No matter how hard he worked, Tyrone knew he would never be as good at football as Johnny.

Then he saw the strongest dinosaur he had ever seen.

"Excuse me," Tyrone said. "You are so strong. Do you play football?"

"Me? Oh, no!" the strong dinosaur said.

"You're very tall. Do you play basketball?" Tyrone asked.

"Goodness, no," she said. "I'm working out
so I can be a stronger dancer."

Tyrone could not believe his ears. "You're a dancer?"
he gasped. "Dancing is *my* dream," he said softly.

"That's your dream?" Johnny asked. "To dance?"

"Well," said Tyrone, "I guess, I mean, it sort of . . . is. . . ."

"If that's your dream," Johnny said, "you have to go for it!"
"Really, Johnny?" said Tyrone.
"Really, Tyrone," said Johnny.

"I'm Brontorina," said the strong dinosaur. "And these are my friends. We are learning to dance at Madame Lucille's Outdoor Dance Academy for Girls and Boys and Dinosaurs and Cows. Come with us, Tyrone."

"I would love to, Brontorina," Tyrone said.

And off they went.

"This is Tyrone," Brontorina told Madame Lucille. "He wants to learn to dance."

"Welcome, Tyrone!" said Madame Lucille. "Music, Magnolia!"

"You are a very good—and very strong—dancer!"
Madame Lucille told Tyrone.

"Do you really think so?" asked Tyrone.

"I do!" said Madame Lucille. "Would you like to study with us? You will need to work hard, but there could be a very special part for you in our next recital."

"Oh, I will work very hard," said Tyrone. "Thank you, Madame Lucille!"

When it came time for the recital, no one cheered louder than Tyrone's family.

Tyrone was so happy, he thought his heart would burst. He knew he would always be happy as long as he could dance.

And it all began with a dream.